Courtney

John Burningham

Other books by John Burningham

Avocado Baby	Simp	*Little Books*
Aldo	Seasons	The Dog
Courtney	Time to get out of the Bath, Shirley	The School
ABC	Come Away from the Water, Shirley	The Friend
Albert	Would You Rather?	The Baby
Cloudland	The Shopping Basket	The Cupboard
Grandpa	Where's Julius?	The Snow
Trubloff	Humbert	The Rabbit
Humbert	Oi! Get off our Train	The Blanket
Harquin	Mr Gumpy's Outing	
Borka	Mr Gumpy's Motor Car	

A Red Fox Book

Published by Random House Children's Books
20 Vauxhall Bridge Road, London SW1V 2SA

A division of Random House UK Ltd
London Melbourne Sydney Auckland
Johannesburg and agencies throughout the world

1 3 5 7 9 10 8 6 4 2

First published in Great Britain by
Jonathan Cape Ltd 1994
Red Fox edition 1999

Printed in Singapore

RANDOM HOUSE UK Limited Reg. No. 954009

ISBN 0 09 966681 2

'We would really like to have a dog,' the children said. 'Our house would be much better with a dog. The dog would guard the house and it could play with us.'

'There are lots of lovely dogs at the Dogs' Home. Can't we please have one?'

'Dogs need feeding and walking.'

'And they make a mess everywhere.'

'We will walk the dog and feed it.'

'And we will clean up the mess.'

'Please, can we?'

'Oh, very well then, if you must.'

'Make sure it's a proper dog. One with a pedigree.
And remember you'll both have to take care of it.'

The children looked at lots of dogs. None of them seemed to
be what they wanted.

'Have you a dog that nobody wants?' they asked the man.
'All the dogs we have seen will find homes easily.'
'We do have a dog called Courtney,' said the man. 'Nobody
wants Courtney.'

'We don't know anything about him,' said the man. 'We don't know where he came from. Nobody wants him and he's an old dog.'

'We want Courtney,' said the children, and they took him home.

'What on earth have you got there?' said the parents. 'Why
didn't you get a proper dog? He's old and he's a
mongrel, not a pedigree like we said.'
'But Courtney's lovely,' said the children.

'Well, it's getting late now and you must be going to bed. Courtney will have to sleep in the kitchen.'

The next morning the children raced down to the kitchen to see their new dog but Courtney was not there.

'We said the dog was no good. These mongrels, you can't rely
on them. Why on earth didn't you get a proper dog
like we said?'

That afternoon, Courtney came back dragging a large trunk behind him.

Once in the house, he opened the trunk, put on a chef's hat and apron, and immediately began to cook a delicious meal.

He changed into waiter's clothes and served the family round the table.

Courtney then played the violin while the family finished the meal.

Out of his trunk, he took some things to juggle with and
entertain the baby.

Sometimes Courtney would meet other dogs in the park.

But most of the time he spent with the family.

One day, the house caught fire and the family were outside waiting for the fire brigade to arrive.

'Where's Courtney?' said one of the children.
'Where's my baby?' shrieked the mother.

Then they saw Courtney climbing down the ladder, holding the baby.

The fire was put out and the house was soon repaired and the family were able to carry on living as usual.

One morning they came downstairs and Courtney was not there. The children looked everywhere, but they could not find Courtney or his trunk. 'We told you the dog was no good,' said the parents. 'If they are not thoroughbreds you cannot rely on them.'

The children went to the police station. 'We've lost our dog. He's quite old, with big eyebrows. He can play the violin, cook wonderful dinners and he juggles to entertain the baby.' 'I'll certainly let you know if an old dog with big eyebrows who can play the violin, cook wonderful dinners and juggle to keep the baby amused is handed in,' said the policeman.

That summer, the family went to the seaside for their holidays
and they took a boat with them.

Every day the children went out in the boat. The boat was always tied to a rock with a long piece of rope so it would not drift out to sea. But on the last day something awful happened . . .

The rope broke. They lost the oars.

The boat drifted out to sea. 'Somebody help us!' cried the mother.

The boat had drifted almost out of sight. Then suddenly there was a tug.

The boat was being pulled by something.

Toward the shore.

They never did find out who or what it was that had pulled their boat back to shore.

I wonder what it could have been.